CALGARY PUBLIC LIBRARY

SEP   2019

NOTE FROM THE AUTHOR:

"Uh-oh, Rollo!" is a phrase that my partner, Anna Dewdney, used to say around the house when the real Rollo was up to his usual mischief. The inspiration for this book is from her.

ABOUT THE AUTHOR:

Reed Duncan is an author as well as a former reading instructor, teacher, and school administrator. He lives in Vermont. The Rollo stories are based on Reed and his real-life, rambunctious bulldog.

W

PENGUIN WORKSHOP

An Imprint of Penguin Random House LLC, New York

Penguin supports copyright. Copyright fuels creativity, encourages diverse voices, promotes free speech, and creates a vibrant culture. Thank you for buying an authorized edition of this book and for complying with copyright laws by not reproducing, scanning, or distributing any part of it in any form without permission. You are supporting writers and allowing Penguin to continue to publish books for every reader.

Text copyright © 2019 by Reed Duncan. Illustrations copyright © 2019 by Penguin Random House LLC. All rights reserved. Published by Penguin Workshop, an imprint of Penguin Random House LLC, New York. PENGUIN and PENGUIN WORKSHOP are trademarks of Penguin Books Ltd, and the W colophon is a registered trademark of Penguin Random House LLC. Manufactured in China.

Visit us online at www.penguinrandomhouse.com.

Library of Congress Cataloging-in-Publication Data is available upon request.

ISBN 9781524792435   10 9 8 7 6 5 4 3 2 1

UH-OH, ROLLO!

by REED DUNCAN
illustrated by KEITH FRAWLEY

PENGUIN WORKSHOP

Rollo is a good dog.

He loves to play.

But sometimes he does things that get him into trouble.

Rollo loves to dig,
but sometimes he digs too much.

ROLLO,
NO!

He does not wipe his paws
before he comes back inside.

ROLL-O . . .

Rollo loves to chew,
but sometimes he chews
things he should not.

Rollo loves to climb,
but sometimes he climbs
where he should not.

16

SILLY ROLL-O . . .

Rollo likes to chase things.

But sometimes he chases
things he should not.

UH-OH, ROLLO!

Rollo loves to eat.

But sometimes he eats
things he should not.

Rollo feels sick.
Poor Rollo.

But there's one thing that Rollo
loves to do the most.

And that's to say he's sorry.